AND THEN COMES
Christmas

To Kaylan, my editor; Nancy, my wife;
June and Nancy, my sisters; and Ruth and Roy for my Christmases.
T. B.

For Harry and Hugo, and all of the Christmases we've spent together,
and all of the trees you have given names to. I love you.
J. C.

First published 2014 by Walker Books Ltd
87 Vauxhall Walk, London SE11 5HJ

2 4 6 8 10 9 7 5 3 1

Text © 2014 Tom Brenner
Illustrations © 2014 Jana Christy

The right of Tom Brenner and Jana Christy to be identified as author and illustrator respectively of this work
has been asserted by them in accordance with the Copyright, Designs and Patents Act 1988

This book has been typeset in Warnock

Printed in China

British Library Cataloguing in Publication Data:
a catalogue record for this book is available from the British Library

ISBN 978-1-4063-5782-0

www.walker.co.uk

AND THEN COMES
Christmas

TOM BRENNER

illustrated by **JANA CHRISTY**

WALKER BOOKS
AND SUBSIDIARIES

LONDON • BOSTON • SYDNEY • AUCKLAND

WHEN the days barely start before they're over again,
and red berries blaze against green shrubs,
and bare branches rake across the sky ...

THEN hang up boughs of fir or spruce or pine,
dotted with cones and bits of holly, welcoming winter.

WHEN frost glistens on pastures and fence posts,
and icy grass crunches underfoot,
and dark clouds sit low on the horizon …

THEN fill the windows with paper snowflakes and frame the house with coloured lights.

WHEN the red in the thermometer sinks towards the bulb,
and icicles cling to the edges of roofs,
and raindrops shift to feathery flakes …

THEN wrap yourself in layers and tumble out of doors
to romp in snow as smooth as bedcovers.

WHEN elves and reindeer appear in shops,
and small trains race through toy villages,
and piles of presents nestle in cotton drifts ...

Santa →

THEN hop from foot to foot,
waiting to sit on Santa's knee.

WHEN cardboard boxes arrive and are quickly hidden,
and the neighbourhood blinks with twinkly lights,
and empty spaces turn into forests ...

THEN head out and wander along the rows
in search of the perfect tree.

WHEN Daddy brings it into the house,
and Mummy gets it to stand straight and tall,
and the room fills with that sweet piny scent ...

THEN loop lights in graceful arcs,
place shiny baubles just so,
and settle the angel on the very top.

WHEN the winter holiday is just hours away,
and the programmes and concerts are over,
and Mummy's and Daddy's presents
are done …

THEN sneak your treasures home,
and cut and wrap and tape with care,
and finish them off with ribbons and bows.

WHEN the days in December reach twenty-four,
and the sweet smell of baking fills the house,
and neighbours drop by with home-made goodies …

THEN hang your stockings where they can't be missed
and tuck your presents under the tree.

Set out biscuits and milk and plenty of carrots.

And with the sound of carols fading away,
snuggle down in bed to hear those
familiar words –
"'Twas the night before..."

WHEN one by one the lights go out,
and the whispering and shushing dwindle away,
and the whole world seems to be waiting …

THEN, lo and behold, it's Christmas morning!

The milk and biscuits and carrots are gone!

The stockings are stuffed full!

And presents spill out from under the tree, begging to be opened!

AND WHEN Daddy lights the fire,
and oohs and aahs and thank-yous sound around the room,
and wrapping paper covers the floor …

THEN gather at the table …

and bask in the magic of Christmas.